Carlos & Carmen

The Fun Fort

by Kirsten McDonald
illustrated by Fátima Anaya

Calico Kid

An Imprint of Magic Wagon
abdopublishing.com

For MSH, the builder —KKM

For Memito, my beautiful nephew, who has brought fun to my life.—FA

abdopublishing.com

THIS BOOK CONTAINS
RECYCLED MATERIALS

Written by Kirsten McDonald
Illustrated by Fátima Anaya
Edited by Heidi M.D. Elston
Design Contributors: Christina Doffing & Candice Keimig

Publisher's Cataloging-in-Publication Data

Names: McDonald, Kirsten, author. | Anaya, Fátima, illustrator.
Title: The fun fort / by Kirsten McDonald; illustrated by Fátima Anaya.
Description: Minneapolis, Minnesota : Magic Wagon, 2018. | Series: Carlos & Carmen
Summary: The Garcia's new refrigerator comes in a big box. Carlos and Carmen turn the box into a rocket, then a submarine. Then the twins finally decide to make the box a fort. But it's a crumpled fort. It's a flat fort. Discover how Carlos and Carmen don't let a flattened box ruin their fun!
Identifiers: LCCN 2017946754 | ISBN 9781532130335 (lib.bdg.) | ISBN 9781532130939 (ebook) | ISBN 9781532131233 (Read-to-me ebook)
Subjects: LCSH: Hispanic American families--Juvenile fiction. | Imagination in children--Juvenile fiction. | Brothers and sisters--Juvenile fiction. | Fortification--Juvenile fiction.
Classification: DDC [E]--dc23
LC record available at https://lccn.loc.gov/2017946754

Table of Contents

Chapter 1
Big, Brown Plans

Mamá and Papá pushed the big, brown box into the kitchen. They were excited about their brand-new refrigerator.

Carlos and Carmen were excited too.

"Try not to scrape it, por favor," said Carlos.

"Be careful as you get it out, por favor," said Carmen.

"Mis hijos," said Mamá. "I had no idea you were so excited about our new refrigerator."

Carmen tilted her head to the side and scrunched up her mouth. Carlos shrugged his shoulders and wrinkled his nose. Neither twin said a thing.

Mamá stopped pushing. "What's going on?" she asked.

"A new fridge is nice," said Carlos.

"But a big, brown box is even better," Carmen finished.

"What will you do with the caja?" asked Papá.

"We've got plans," said Carlos.

"Big, brown plans," added Carmen.

"In that case," said Mamá, "let's get this caja into the backyard."

Carlos and Carmen ran into the backyard. They had crayons, and they had markers. They had big plans, and they had big smiles.

Mamá and Papá carried the box to the middle of the backyard.

Mamá said, "I made a cut here." She pushed on a piece of the box. It opened like a little door.

"Hooray!" shouted Carmen. "Our caja has a door."

"And I made a cut here," said Papá, pushing on the box. The cardboard square swung inside the box like a little window.

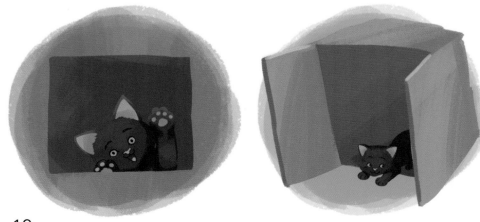

"Double hooray!" shouted Carlos. "Our box has a ventana too!"

Carmen gave Mamá a hug and said, "Gracias, Mamá."

Carlos gave Papá a hug and said, "Gracias, Papá."

"You're welcome," said Mamá and Papá.

Carlos and Carmen tipped the box over. They crawled inside and closed the window and the door.

"On your mark," said Carlos.

"Get set," said Carmen.

"Go!" they both shouted.

Then they rolled inside the box, and the box rolled too. Around and around they went before tumbling out of the box.

The twins looked at the box. It had crumpled corners. It had grass stains. But, it still had lots of fun.

Chapter 2
Big, Brown Fun

Carlos and Carmen went in the little door and opened the window. They drew dials. They drew buttons and throttles.

Then they blasted off in their big, brown rocket. They raced past stars and circled moons.

Finally Carmen stood up and said, "Prepare for splashdown!"

Carlos stood up too. He pressed a drawn-on button. "Ready for splashdown," he said.

The twins rattled the rocket from side to side. They shook the rocket back and forth and back and forth. Until finally, the rocket tumbled over.

"Now it's a submarino," said Carlos.

"¡Mira, Carmen! I can see fish outside my submarine ventana."

"Wait a minute," said Carmen. "No peeking."

Carmen drew as fast as she could. "¡Mira, Carlos!" she said. "There's a shark outside our submarino."

"Good thing the ventanas are really strong," said Carlos.

"Let's use the hatch to see if there's another tiburón," said Carmen.

Carlos and Carmen squeezed through the hatch and looked around.

"Do you see a tiburón?" asked Carmen.

"No, but I do see an island," said Carlos.

"Then let's make this submarino into a fort," said Carmen.

Chapter 3
The Flat Fort

Carlos and Carmen stood the box up. It leaned to the left. It sagged to the right. When Spooky jumped on top, the fort crumpled to the ground.

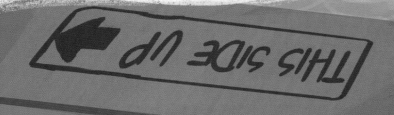

THIS SIDE UP

They tried again and again, but the box would not stand up. The twins looked at the flattened box.

"It's not a very good fortaleza," said Carmen sadly.

"That's for sure," said Carlos with a sigh. He nudged the flattened box with his foot. It was a problem. A big, flat, brown problem.

"We need something strong to fix our fortaleza," said Carmen.

"We need something strong enough for Spooky to sit on," said Carlos.

The twins thought and thought. They thought of all the things Spooky liked to sit on. Then Carlos looked at Carmen, and Carmen looked at Carlos.

"Are you thinking what I'm thinking?" they asked at the same time. And because they were twins, they were.

Carlos and Carmen ran to the back deck. They peered underneath it. They saw lots of things Spooky liked to sit on.

They saw their old plastic picnic table. They saw two folding chairs and the lid for a big, plastic bin. They even saw their old, blue wading pool.

Chapter 4

The Perfect Fort

Mamá and Papá went outside.
They looked for the twins, and they
looked for the box.

27

"Mis hijos!" called Mamá. "Where are you?"

"We're inside our fortaleza!" Carlos and Carmen answered.

"I can't see a fort," said Papá.

"Surprise!" the twins shouted as they scrambled out of their fort.

Mamá and Papá looked at the twins. They looked at the pile of junk. And, they looked at the upside down pool on top of it all.

"What happened to the caja?" asked Mamá.

"First it went around and around," said Carmen.

"Then it blasted into space," said Carlos.

"Then it got chased by a tiburón," added Carmen.

"And now it's our fortaleza," finished Carlos.

"Hmm," said Mamá. "I thought your fort would be more brown."

"It used to be," said Carmen. "But now it's not a brown fort."

"And, I thought your fortaleza would be more boxy," said Papá.

"It used to be," said Carlos. "But now it's not a boxy fort."

Then the twins smiled. They said, "Now it's just a really fun fort."

Spanish to English

caja – box
fortaleza – fort
gracias – thank you
Mamá – Mommy
¡Mira! – Look!
mis hijos – my children
Papá – Daddy
por favor – please
submarino – submarine
tiburón – shark
ventana – window

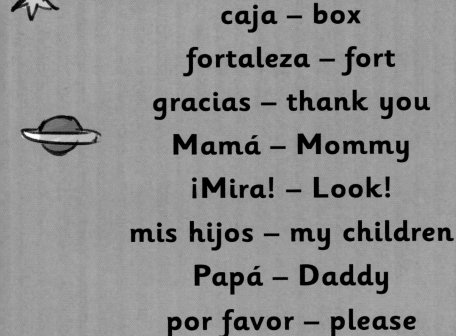